Order this book online at www.trafford.com
or email orders@trafford.com

Most Trafford titles are also available at major online book retailers.

Trafford www.trafford.com
PUBLISHING
North America & international
toll-free: 844 688 6899 (USA & Canada)
fax: 812 355 4082

Our mission is to efficiently provide the world's finest, most comprehensive book publishing service, enabling every author to experience success. To find out how to publish your book, your way, and have it available worldwide, visit us online at www.trafford.com

Because of the dynamic nature of the Internet, any web addresses or links contained in this book may have changed since publication and may no longer be valid. The views expressed in this work are solely those of the author and do not necessarily reflect the views of the publisher, and the publisher hereby disclaims any responsibility for them.

Any people depicted in stock imagery provided by Getty Images are models, and such images are being used for illustrative purposes only.
Certain stock imagery © Getty Images.

ISBN: 978-1-6987-0364-0 (sc)
ISBN: 978-1-6987-0363-3 (e)

Library of Congress Control Number: 2021909619

Print information available on the last page.

Trafford rev. 05/11/2021

The adventures of

Spotty
and
Sunny.

Book 5: Summer camp in the Everglades.

Summer camp in the Everglades.

Author/Pharmacist

SAISNATH BAIJOO

Mom rushes into her kid's bedroom. "Wake up, my four sleepy heads. I am excited. Today is the first day of summer camp and you are late. It's time to rise and shine. Are you ready to have fun, fun and more fun?" Mom says happily.

Yes, mommy. I like summer camps, but a girl must get her beauty sleep."

Mommy jokes, "I heard Spotty, Sunny and all their friends will be there."

Jas jumps out the bed, "Really, I never met Spotty and Sunny. Let us go now."

Davin, Dominic and Jordi shouts together, "Yes. We love Spotty, Sunny and all their friends. They are fun."

Jordi yawns. "Mom, is Grandpa taking us to summer camp? He always takes us to McDonalds for yummy food."

Mom smiles. She points to the bathroom. "Yes, but first, brush your teeth, take a bath, change your clothes, and eat your breakfast. Don't forget to wash your hands after. Let us get moving now."

Mom claps her hands. Everyone rushes to the bathroom, changes their clothes, and eats their tasty breakfast. They wash their hands again.

Grandpa blows his car horn. He is waiting in his car. Mum and Dad comes to see their kids off to summer camp. They kiss Grandpa.

Jas rushes to Grandpa's car, "I want to sit in the front seat and play my music."

Grandpa says nicely, "Kids, you must take turns sitting in the front seat. Learn to share."

Grandpa smiles, "Good morning, kids. Put on your seat belts.

Everyone answers together. "Good morning Grandpa."

Jas says, "Grandpa, can we get McDonalds after summer camp? I know, we will be hungry. Please, please."

All the boys answer at the same time, "Yes, please."

"Okay kids." Grandpa adds while driving his car.

Davin touches Grandpa and jokes, "Grandpa, can your old car go any faster. We would like to see Spotty and Sunny.

"Safety comes first. We must obey the speed limit." Grandpa says with a broad smile.

Suddenly, a small dog runs in front of their car. Grandpa stops suddenly. He rushes outside his car. He raises the dog and brings her inside the car.

Everyone is excited. They have a new friend.

Dominic makes a sad face to Grandpa, "Can we keep him pretty please? She is all alone and hungry. She is mine. Her name shall be Cuddles."

Davin points to the frightened dog. "She is lost. She has no friends."

Jas adds smartly, "Grandpa's heart is made of gold. Pretty please, can I keep him?"

Grandpa scratches his head, "Yes for now. Maybe."

Davin jumps in, "Let us go home. We can play with Cuddles our new friend. Can we, can we Grandpa?"

Grandpa laughs, "No, Davin. Summer camp is fun. Cuddles can sit in the back seat."

Jas smartly says, "Does anyone want to come in the front seat? It is better."

My dog eyes are green. His hairs are black, white, and gray. His tongue is pink." says Jordi as he hugs his new friend.

Grandpa says, "We will be late for summer camp. We must go now. I will take care of Cuddles."

They reach summer camp in the Everglades. Everyone is sad to leave Cuddles, their new best friend.

At the camp door Miss Crabby greets them with a crabby hug. "Welcome to summer camp. Get dressed for swimming. A race is about to start now."

In the swimming pool lanes, they meet Dolph, the playful dolphin, Spotty, Sunny, Mr. Turtle, Jorge, Jean, Kim, Mrs. Crabby, the singing crab. They greet everyone.

Davin and Dominic raise their hands. "Can
we enter the swimming race?

Sure, there is room for two more swimmers."
says Dan, the tall and strong lifeguard.

Dominic and Davin jump quickly in the pool. Dan checks the
swimmers. "Let me see. There are 1,2,3,4,5,6,7,8,9,10 lanes
for 10 swimmers. First, you swim east to west and back again,
west to east. You must stay in your lane. Good luck, everyone."

Dan blows his whistle to start the race. Dolph takes an early lead followed Sunny, Snapper, Carlos, Kim, and Jean. Dolph turns back quickly to win the race. Dolph flips in and out of the water in joy.

Dan says, "Everyone's a winner for taking part in this race."

Mr. Turtle is the last one in the race. He raises his hand. "Yes, I am the slowest, but I am a winner."

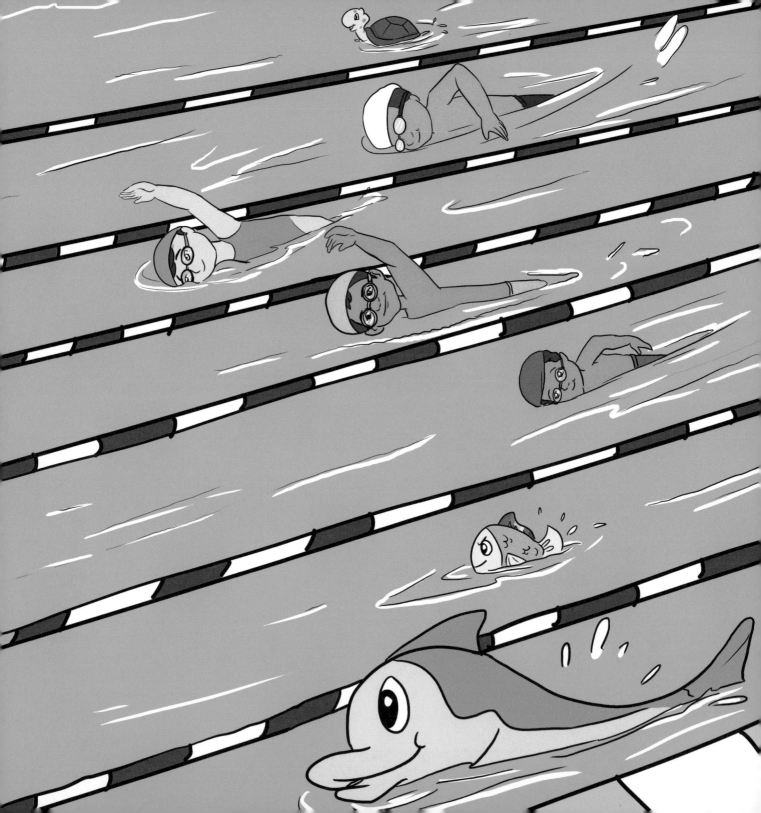

Miss Snapper raises her colorful fin and shouts. "Are you ready for a veggie lunch? We have veggies, burgers and tacos. Is everyone hungry?"

Spotty says, "I love my veggies." Everyone agrees.

Dan blows his whistle loudly. "Kids follow me in a single line to the lunchroom. Wash your hands with soap and water."

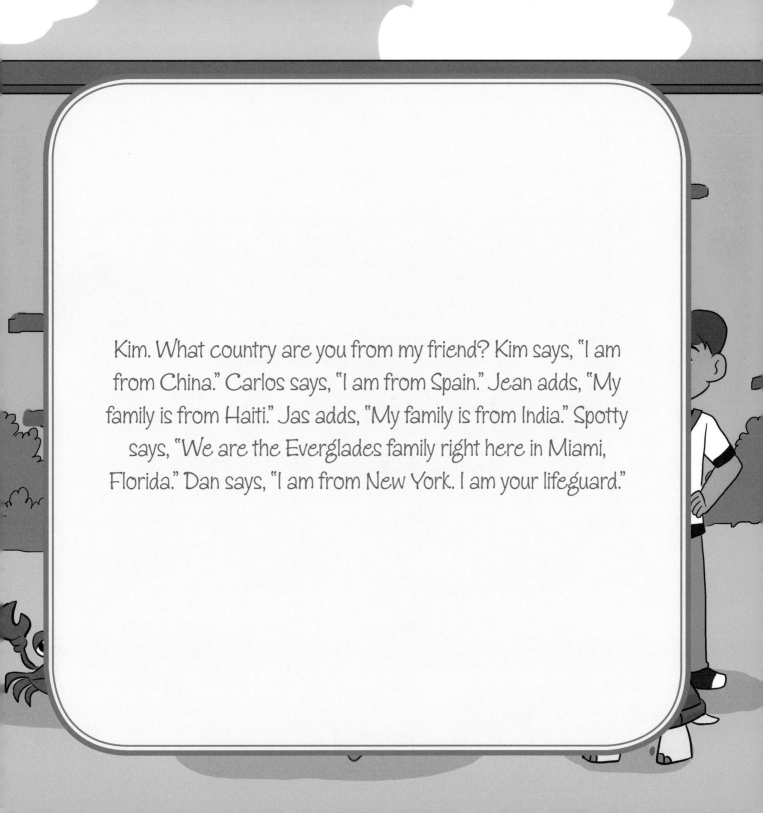

Kim. What country are you from my friend? Kim says, "I am from China." Carlos says, "I am from Spain." Jean adds, "My family is from Haiti." Jas adds, "My family is from India." Spotty says, "We are the Everglades family right here in Miami, Florida." Dan says, "I am from New York. I am your lifeguard."

Sunny says to everyone, "Love and life have no boundaries. We are all God's creations. We are one big, happy family. We love our summer camp."

Sunny says, "Yes, we are different, but our hearts beat the same. Everyone enjoyed summer camp. They came every day to be one happy family.

Printed in the United States
by Baker & Taylor Publisher Services